This igloo book
belongs to:

....

igloobooks

Published in 2020
First published in the UK by Igloo Books Ltd
An imprint of Igloo Books Ltd
Cottage Farm, NN6 0BJ, UK
Owned by Bonnier Books
Sveavägen 56, Stockholm, Sweden
www.igloobooks.com

1220 001
2 4 6 8 10 9 7 5 3 1
ISBN 978-1-83903-464-0

Written by Stephanie Moss
Illustrated by Claudia Ranucci

Designed by Laura Chamberlain
Edited by Hannah Campling

Printed and manufactured in China

WANTED
PANDA

igloobooks

I WANT A

PANDA!

What's that?

you say.

It's a cute, cuddly friend
I can play with all day!

Erm... nice cat?
But not even close.

EEK!

No, thank you.

I want a panda.

There's no need to glare.
Okay, I'll tell you.
A panda's a BEAR.

Getting warmer!

But no, that's just
a teddy bear.

I want a panda.

You say,

Tell me more.

This kind of bear really
loves the outdoors.

Wrong again.
That's a grizzly bear.

RUN!

I want a panda.

Still you don't know?
Well, it's black and white
from its head to its toes.

Okay, it likes sleeping and lounging about.

No... but can I keep hiiiim?

I want a panda.
No, don't give up yet!

A panda is

giant

and makes a great pet!

Good, we're back to bears.
But this bear's only white!

Remember what we talked about...
he likes the outdoors, cute and cuddly,
black AND white?

I want a panda.

You've got this, be strong!
This hungry bear loves
to eat all day long.

NO, silly! Now you're getting totally confused.
You've forgotten about the bear part again.

Oh, did I tell you
he eats bamboo... ?

I want a panda!

I've got it!

you cry.

I take a deep breath
and I open my eyes...